JOHANNA WRIGHT

Bandits

A NEAL PORTER BOOK
ROARING BROOK PRESS
NEW YORK

A Neal Porter Book

Published by Roaring Brook Press

Roaring Brook Press is a division of Holtzbrinck Publishing Holdings Limited Partnership

175 Fifth Avenue, New York, New York 10010

www.roaringbrookpress.com

Library of Congress Cataloging-in-Publication Data

Wright, Johanna.

Bandits / Johanna Wright. — 1st ed.

p. cm.

"A Neal Porter Book."

Summary: Raccoons wreak havoc on a town during the night, rummaging through garbage cans, stealing food, and then running off into the hills to enjoy their loot.

ISBN 978-1-59643-583-4

[1. Raccoon—Fiction.] I. Title.

PZ7.W9496Ban 2011

[E]—dc22

2010027310

Roaring Brook Press books are available for special promotions and premiums.

For details contact: Director of Special Markets, Holtzbrinck Publishers.

First edition 2011

Book design by Jennifer Browne

Printed in April 2011 in China by South China Printing Co. Ltd., Dongguan City, Guangdong Province

1 3 5 7 9 8 6 4 2

For Alden and Myla

When the sun goes down and the moon comes up, beware of the bandits that prowl through the night.

They sneak and they creep.

Doing just what they please.

They snatch and launder whatever they've found.

They baffle the fuzz with each little trick.

But those bandits are careless . . .
leaving clue after clue.

And when they are caught . . .

they will never confess!

Back on the run.

They head for the hills
to split up the loot.

And just as the town is starting to stir . . .

the bandits make their greatest escape.

As the sun starts to rise,
back to their hideout,

to wait for the dawn.

Laying low through the day.

But just until . . .

the sun goes down.

COUNTY
DISCARD
MOOK, ORE.